Fergus
Goes Quackers!

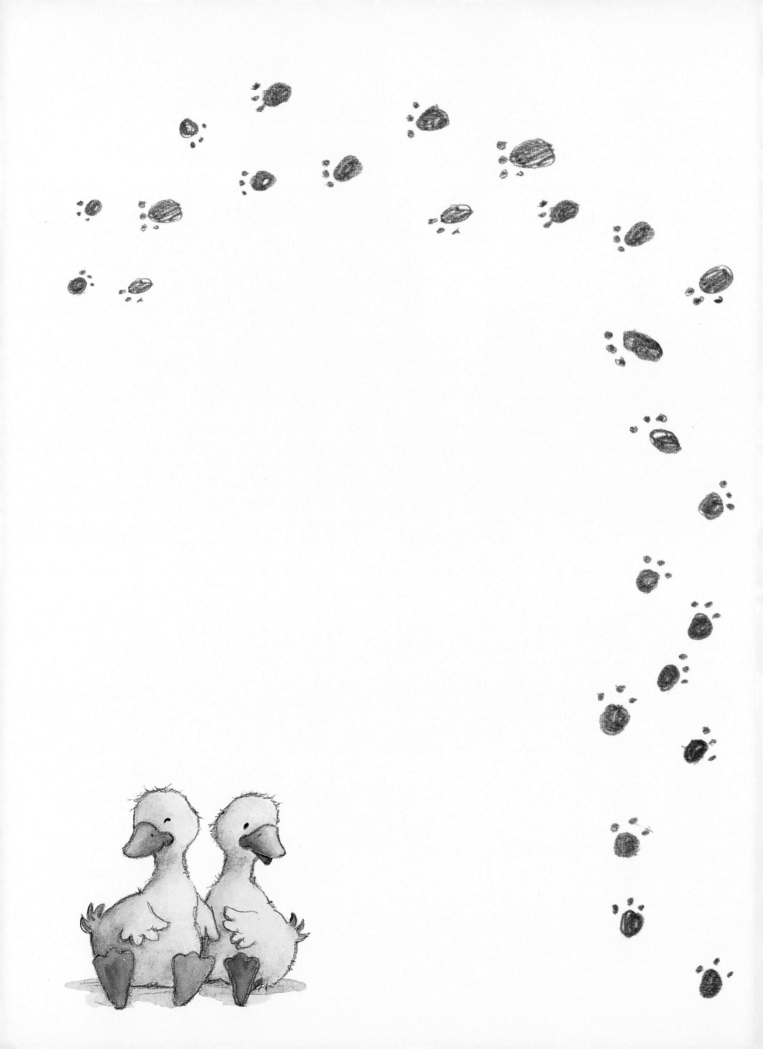

Fergus
Goes Quackers!

For Holly and Olivia

First published in Great Britain in 1998
by Piccadilly Press Ltd,
5 Castle Road, London NW1 8PR
www.piccadillypress.co.uk

Text and illustrations copyright © Tony Maddox, 1998
This edition published 2012

Printed and bound in China

ISBN: 978 1 84812 296 3 (paperback)

1 3 5 7 9 10 8 6 4 2

A catalogue record for this book is available from the British Library

Fergus
Goes Quackers!

Tony Maddox

Piccadilly Press • London

Fergus was on his way back to the farm.
It was getting dark and he was looking forward
to sleeping in his new kennel.

As he walked Fergus could hear
a scuffling sound behind him.
He hurried on.
The scuffling sound was getting nearer.
He stopped and looked nervously over his
shoulder . . . he was being followed
by five baby ducks!

"Woof, Woof!" he said, warning them to go back.
But they took no notice.
Farther on, he tried again. "Woof, Woof!"

It was no use . . . the baby ducks followed him
down the lane, through the farm gate
and into the yard.

It had been a long day and Fergus
was ready for bed.

He went into his
new kennel and settled down
on the warm, woolly blanket.
One by one, the five baby ducks crept in
and snuggled down beside him.
"Woof!" murmured Fergus drowsily.
Soon all of them were asleep.

woof

The next morning, Fergus was woken
by a familiar sound.
"Woof, Woof!"
"That's strange!" he thought.
"That sounds like me . . . but it isn't!
Someone else is making my noise!"
He looked and saw the baby ducks
marching around the farmyard.
"Woof, Woof, Woof!" they chorused.

"They're making the wrong noise!" thought Fergus.
He chased after them, shouting,
"Quack, Quack! It's Quack, Quack!"

The pigs watched in astonishment.
Fergus was going, "Quack!"
and the ducks were going, "Woof!"
"It must be a new game," they thought.
"Let's join in."
So they all went, "Moo, Moo!"

When the hens saw what was happening, they joined in too. "Oink, Oink, Oink!"

cluck
cluck
cluck

And the cow, not wanting to be left out, decided to go, "Cluck, Cluck!"

Everyone was making the wrong noise!

"This is driving me quackers!" thought Fergus.

But a loud "Honk, Honk!" made everyone stop as Farmer Bob's truck came into the yard. He had Mother Duck with him. "Quack, Quack, Quack!" she said when she saw the baby ducks. "Quack, Quack!" they answered excitedly and ran to meet her.

"Well done, Fergus!" said Farmer Bob.
"You found the missing ducklings."
They watched as Mother Duck marched off
towards the duck pond with her five
baby ducks following behind.
"Woof!" Fergus called after them.

"Woof, Woof!" came the reply.

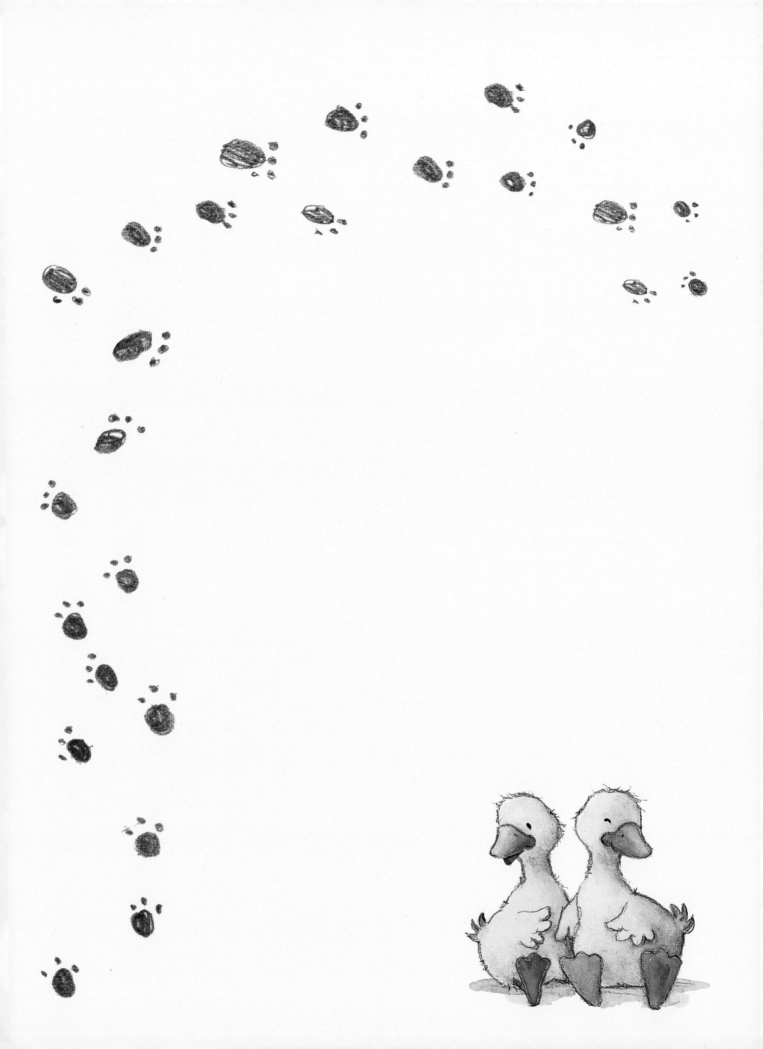